Horse Dreams

Backyard ∩ Horses

Dandi Daley Mackall

author of the bestselling Winnie the Horse Gentler series

Tyndale House Publishers, Inc.

Carol Stream, Illinois

Visit Tyndale's website for kids at www.tyndale.com/kids.

You can contact Dandi Daley Mackall through her website at www.dandibooks.com.

TYNDALE is a registered trademark of Tyndale House Publishers, Inc.

The Tyndale Kids logo is a trademark of Tyndale House Publishers, Inc.

Horse Dreams

Copyright © 2011 by Dandi Daley Mackall. All rights reserved.

Cover photograph of horse copyright © by Brandy Taylor/iStockphoto. All rights reserved.

Cover photograph of fence copyright © by Rowan Butler/iStockphoto. All rights reserved.

Designed by Jacqueline L. Nuñez

Edited by Stephanie Voiland

Unless otherwise indicated, all Scripture quotations are taken from the *Holy Bible*, New Living Translation, copyright © 1996, 2004, 2007 by Tyndale House Foundation. Used by permission of Tyndale House Publishers, Inc., Carol Stream, Illinois 60188. All rights reserved.

Scripture quotations marked NIrV are taken from the Holy Bible, *New International Reader's Version,*® NIrV.® Copyright © 1995, 1996, 1998 by Biblica, Inc.™ Used by permission of Zondervan. All rights reserved worldwide. www.zondervan.com.

For manufacturing information regarding this product, please call 1-800-323-9400.

Library of Congress Cataloging-in-Publication Data

Mackall, Dandi Daley.
   Horse dreams / Dandi Daley Mackall.
      p. cm. – (Backyard horses)
      Summary: Horse-crazy fourth-grader Ellie James constantly dreams about having a horse of her own, and God finally seems to have answered her prayers, but not with the gleaming black stallion she has been longing for.
      ISBN 978-1-4143-3916-0 (sc)
   [1. Horses–Fiction. 2. Schools–Fiction. 3. Christian life–Fiction.] I. Title.
      PZ7.M1905Hno 2011
      [Fic]–dc22   2011008111

Printed in the United States of America

17   16   15   14   13   12   11
 7   6   5   4   3   2   1

To Helen Isabella Hendren, "Ellie"

Backyard horses are the opposite of show horses. They don't have registration papers to prove they're purebred, and they might never win a trophy or ribbon at a horse show. Backyard horses aren't boarded in stables. You can find them in pastures or in backyards. They may be farm horses, fun horses, or simply friends. Backyard horses are often plain and ordinary on the outside . . . but frequently beautiful on the inside.

★ ★ ★

The Lord said to Samuel, "Don't judge by his appearance or height, for I have rejected him. The Lord doesn't see things the way you see them. People judge by outward appearance, but the Lord looks at the heart."

1 Samuel 16:7

1

Imagine!

It's the moment the world has been waiting for. Ellie James enters the horse show ring on her champion stallion, Ellie's Prancing Beauty. The crowd at the Hamilton Royal Horse Show goes wild. They jump to their feet and clap. The lean, black American saddle horse prances past the stands. The judges can't take their eyes off the gorgeous horse and his talented rider. Ellie is dressed in a classic black riding habit and tall

English boots. She is the youngest rider in this year's contest. The horses are called to a canter. Ellie and Prancing Beauty float around the ring. The crowd cheers. The horses line up. The winner is announced. . . .

"Ellie! Miss James!"

I look up. But instead of a judge carrying a trophy for me, it's my fourth-grade teacher standing over my desk.

"Ellie?" Miss Hernandez taps her foot. She frowns at me.

I stare at her for a second before the dream fades. The horse show ring turns back into four walls and twenty-three desks. "Sorry, Miss Hernandez," I mutter.

She keeps staring at me like she's waiting for an answer. "Well?"

But I didn't hear the question. "Um . . . you

see . . ." I am about to give up and admit I've been daydreaming—again. Then I see Colt Stevens. He sits in the desk in front of me. Behind our teacher's back, Colt is using sign language to spell out *r-e-p-o-r-t*.

"Right," I say, getting my brain back. Colt and I both learned how to sign so we could talk with my little brother. But we've discovered that sometimes sign language can come in handy at school too.

Like now. "My report?" I give our teacher my best smile. Colt's older sister says my smile is the best thing about me. That and my eyes. I have big brown eyes, the only thing big about me. I'm the smallest kid in fourth grade.

Miss Hernandez looks surprised that I know what she's talking about. "Yes. Your report."

"I'm going to do my science report on horses," I tell her. I haven't quite figured it out yet. But I know it will have something to do with horses. Everything I do has something to do with horses.

A wave of laughter splashes around our classroom.

Miss Hernandez sighs. She's tall and skinny like a racehorse. The best thing about *her* is her long, black hair that she wears in a ponytail almost every day. "Your science report is about horses?" she asks. "You do remember that the report is on an experiment you choose to do? What will you try to prove *scientifically*?"

I shrug and hope she'll move on to somebody else.

She doesn't. "Ellie?" Our teacher is nice. She says this in a friendly voice. But it still makes my stomach churn.

I bite my bottom lip for three seconds. Then it comes to me. "My experiment will discover the best way for me to get a horse."

A bunch of kids laugh, including Colt.

"That doesn't sound very scientific," Miss

Hernandez says. She crinkles her nose like she's afraid she might be hurting my feelings.

"It *is*, Miss Hernandez," I tell her. "I'm going to report on three ways to get a horse. I'll try all three ways and see which works best."

Her thin lips twist. She's either about to sneeze or about to laugh. "And what exactly are the three ways you plan to try to get this horse?"

"Begging, crying, and praying."

Miss Hernandez turns around, with her back to the class. Her shoulders are shaking. When she faces me again, I'm pretty sure she's trying not to laugh. "Let's talk after school, Ellie. Who wants to go next?"

Ashley Harper raises her hand. She reads her plan right off her paper: "I'm going to do an experiment on how to make a horse's coat shiny. I think molasses added to a horse's breakfast will do it."

Ashley has long, curly blonde hair and blue

eyes. Colt says Ashley will probably be a movie star when she grows up. Her dad—not Ashley—loves horses almost as much as I do. He's the 4-H horsemanship leader. He keeps about a dozen show horses as a hobby. Every Saturday we meet at the Harpers' stable for horsemanship practice, and he lets me ride one of his horses. Ashley can ride any horse she wants from her dad's stable. They're all hers, really. And she still skips half our practices.

Miss Hernandez talks to Ashley about her plan. Ashley has it all worked out. She'll give molasses to some of her horses and not to others. She'll keep track of everything in a notebook that she shows our teacher.

I try to listen to other people's ideas. Colt plans to experiment with kites and keys and lightning. Miss Hernandez wants to make sure he does it safely, but I can tell she's crazy about the idea. But it sounds like cheating to me because Ben Franklin did it first.

It's hard to stay tuned in to our class. My brain keeps wanting to change the channel. Seth is talking too fast about his basketball experiment. Something about balls with different amounts of air in them. He gets so excited that it's hard to keep up with him. His words turn into a buzz inside my head.

So I turn to the window.

Colt teases me about sleeping in class, but I don't. I dream in class, but I don't sleep.

I dream horses. I don't just dream *about* horses. I dream up horses so real I can smell horse. Horse is the best scent in the whole world. They could put that stuff into perfume bottles and make a fortune. Or candles. Maybe I'll do that when I grow up. Then I'd have enough money to buy all the horses I want.

I dream horses at night too. Maybe it's because every single night before I go to sleep, I pray that God will give me a horse. I've prayed that same prayer as long as I can remember. I'll be 10 in a few months, and still no horse.

I tune in to my classroom again. Larissa Richland is explaining how she's going to prove that hot air is lighter than cold air. Or the other way around.

My head turns back to the window even though I don't tell it to.

I know every inch of the school yard outside this window. A green shrub with shiny, pointy leaves grows under the window ledge. Then there's grass and dirt. One wall of our red brick school sticks out on the left. I can see a maple tree just past the wall.

Out a little farther is the flag pole. I imagine riding to school on a beautiful black stallion and tying my horse to the pole. I picture myself slipping down from a shiny English saddle, then hugging my horse's neck before jogging in for class.

In the middle of the Hamilton Elementary School lawn, a sign says, "Welcome!" Sometimes it announces things, like visitors and days off school.

Now I imagine that school is over and I'm sitting on my black stallion.

I'm wearing a black velvet riding helmet and tall black boots. My coat tails fly behind me as my horse and I gallop toward the welcome sign. The sign says, "Go, Ellie!" because the whole school is counting on me to win the Hamilton Royal Horse Show.

As I gallop toward the sign, students watch from their classroom windows. My horse picks up speed. We close in on the sign. It's our jump. I imagine my horse springing off the ground. Up, up, up we sail. Clouds

circle us. We clear the sign and thump to
the ground without losing stride.

I glance over my shoulder at the cheer-
ing crowd of students. I wave. I see my little
brother, Ethan, standing nearby and grin-
ning proudly. I give him the I love you
sign—outside fingers up, thumb to the side.
He returns the sign. Then I turn—

But wait. Another horse is coming. A shaggy horse, covered with mud. It trots one way, then the other. It zigzags like it's lost. I'm not sure what color it is. But I think it's spotted. A pinto? One blob of spot looks like a crooked saddle. The horse is so skinny. It gallops up a side street and disappears.

But it was there.

It was real.

"Miss Hernandez!" I cry, turning back to my classroom.

Miss Hernandez is writing on the whiteboard. She stops in the middle of a word. "Ellie? What's the matter?"

I can hardly get the words out. My throat is dry. I point to the window. "Out there!"

"What? What is it?" our teacher asks.

"I saw a horse!"

2

Trouble

"Ellie James," our teacher says, laying down her marker. "What did you just say?"

"A horse!" I exclaim. "I saw a horse! Right out there!" I point to where I saw it. But of course, the horse isn't there anymore. It has galloped off by now.

Our whole class groans.

"Didn't anybody else see that horse?" I ask. "It was right there in the street."

Larissa rolls her eyes. Her green eyes and

short red hair make me think of a fox. Plus, she can be sly like a fox. She also happens to be the tallest girl in both fourth grades. It's hard to think of the best thing about Larissa, but I guess it would have to be that she has a beautiful horse that she gets to show all over Missouri.

Larissa leans over and whispers something to Ashley.

Our classmate Rashawn tilts her head. I can tell she feels sorry for me.

Sarah, a friend from Sunday school, makes a face at me. I think she's warning me to back off.

"I *did* see it!" I shout, even though I know I'm supposed to use my inside voice.

"Yeah, right," Larissa mutters.

"That's enough," our teacher says. "I guess I'd better take a look." She walks to the window and peers out. "Where exactly is this horse?"

"In the street, in front of school," I explain.

Miss Hernandez stares out the window. Her ponytail swishes like a horse's tail. "I don't see anything, Ellie." She turns and smiles at me. "Are you sure it wasn't your imagination?"

"I'm sure! I saw a horse! I think it was a pinto. You know, a spotted horse. Why won't anybody believe me?"

"Uh . . . maybe because you're always seeing horses?" Larissa says.

Ashley and some of the kids in her row laugh.

"I said that's enough." Miss Hernandez frowns at them. "Let's get back to work." She glances at me. "Ellie, you and I can talk about this after school."

"Ooooh."

"Uh-oh."

"Dumm-duh-dum-dum."

I keep my head down. If I stare hard enough at my desk, I can keep from crying. I think.

"No more talking. Got it?" Miss Hernandez means business. "Copy your assignment from the board, everybody."

Without turning around, Colt raises his hands where I can see them. Then he signs, *Way to go.*

"I said no talking. That goes for you, too, Colt." Miss Hernandez is good. She can't read sign language, but she sure knows it when she sees it.

I get out my notebook and copy the assignment. But I can't stop thinking about that horse. Our town, Hamilton, Missouri, isn't very big. We have only about two thousand people. So I know most of the horses around here.

But I don't remember seeing a scroungy pinto like that one.

We should all be out looking for that poor, lost horse. I raise my hand. Then I put it back down. I know Miss Hernandez doesn't believe I saw a horse. Nobody in this whole classroom believes me. Nobody in this entire school will believe I saw a wild horse run by, no matter what I say.

It's a horrible feeling when the only one who believes you is you.

Finally the bell rings. I grab my books and hurry toward the door. Miss Hernandez stops me before I get there.

"Ellie? Don't forget. We need to talk."

"Oh yeah," I answer.

Miss Hernandez and I wait until everybody else files out of the classroom. I study the coffee mug holding down a stack of papers on her desk. The mug reads, *#1 Teacher*. Larissa gave it to our teacher the first day of class. That was before any of us knew that she really is the #1 teacher.

I lean against the big wooden desk. But I have to be careful because of the stacks of books and papers piled all over it. That's one of the things I like about Miss Hernandez. Ms. Jones, my third-grade teacher, had to have everything in perfect order. She expected us to be perfect too.

Miss Hernandez closes the door after the last kid is out. It's just the two of us. I think I'm in big trouble.

"Have a seat, Ellie," she says. She sits in her chair again and opens her desk drawer. "Want a peppermint?" She hands me a red-and-white peppermint candy.

I unwrap it. We each pop one into our mouths. "Thank you," I say, and my voice cracks. I settle into the big chair beside her desk.

She sighs. "So what are you and I going to do about daydreaming?"

"Do you daydream too?" I ask.

She grins. "As a matter of fact, I do. Sometimes I daydream I'm on a beach, lying under the sun. Only I make sure not to daydream at school."

I look down at the paper clips on her desk.

I know she means that I shouldn't daydream at school either. "I'm sorry."

"I know," she says. "It's just that when you imagined seeing that horse this afternoon, you—"

"No! I didn't imagine that!"

"Now, Ellie," she says.

I shake my head. "I saw it. A muddy, scraggly horse trotting this way and that, like it was lost."

My teacher takes in a big breath and holds it. I think she's counting to 10 before answering. My mom does that a lot.

"I'm not sure how to handle this," Miss Hernandez begins. "Disturbing the class is one thing. Not knowing the difference between what's real and what's not . . . that's another."

"But I—!"

She holds up one finger to stop me. It works.

"I think you should go home and give this some more thought." Miss Hernandez scribbles something on a piece of paper and puts the paper into an envelope. On the outside she writes, *Mr. and Mrs. James.*

She hands me the envelope. "See that your parents get this note, okay? I think it would be a good idea for all of us to talk about this together."

I think it would be a lousy idea. A king-sized, rotten, crummy, superbad idea.

But I don't say so because I'm already in enough trouble.

3

Hope

Colt is waiting outside for me. "So? What happened?"

I shrug and keep walking. "Miss Hernandez doesn't believe I saw a horse."

"No kidding." He falls in step beside me.

"Great. You don't believe me either?" I wish I'd never seen that ugly horse. Still, I can't stop worrying about it.

Colt glances around. I know he's looking for Dylan and Brooks. Colt and I have walked home together almost every day since kindergarten. Now all of a sudden it's a crime if his buddies see us together?

Sometimes I just don't get people. Horses make much more sense. Once two horses partner up, they stay friends forever, no matter what other horses come into the herd. I guess that's why they call it *horse sense*–horses just seem to have a lot more common sense than people do.

"I believe you think you saw a horse," Colt says. "And I believe you're going to be in a mess of trouble if your dad has to go to school again because you were daydreaming."

He's right about that one. My dad hates school conferences. He went to my school when he was a kid. He hated conferences then too.

"So?" Colt elbows me. "Did Miss Hernandez call your mom?"

"No."

"That's good," Colt says. "Last time I got in trouble, Miss Hernandez called my mother. Or tried to, anyway. She finally gave up and left a voice mail, which was bad enough."

I'm barely listening to Colt. I'm too busy imagining my dad at another parent-teacher conference. "She gave me a note for my parents."

"A note? What does it say?" Colt keeps walking beside me. But now he's turned toward me, looking for the note. I've already stuffed it into my backpack.

"I'm not opening the note, Colt."

We reach the corner. From here we can either keep going straight another block or cut through the ball field. I take the path through the field.

Colt follows me. "Can't you just tell them your imagination got the best of you?"

I stop so suddenly that Colt trips over me. "Colt Stevens, did you hear me say I *saw*—not imagined—a scrawny, spotted horse?"

"Yeah. But you're always imagining you see horses."

"True," I admit. "And what kind of horses do I imagine?"

"How should I know?" He tugs at the straps of his backpack.

"Beautiful horses. That's what kind!"

Colt frowns, a sure sign he's thinking. "What are you getting at?"

"In all the years you've known me, have I ever once told you about an imaginary *ugly* horse?"

"No," he admits.

"When I imagine a horse, I imagine a gorgeous show horse. A Hamilton Royal champion horse."

I can tell by his raised eyebrows and half-open mouth that I've finally gotten through to him.

"Colt, heads up!"

Out of nowhere, a ball whizzes by, inches

from my nose. I wheel around and see Dylan and Brooks running toward us.

Behind me, Colt scrambles for the ball. "Back at ya!" he hollers. He fires the ball at Brooks.

I keep walking home . . . alone.

I used to feel sorry for my little brother because most people will never know what he's saying. But at least the people who can understand Ethan always believe him.

★ ★ ★

Mom's car isn't in the driveway. Dad's car is probably in our one-car garage. I squint into the picture window and see my dad sitting at the dining table. His back is to me. Dad calls our dining room his office when we're not eating there.

I'm pretty sure I can make it to my room without being seen.

With the courage of a wild stallion, I slip inside the house. Silently I ease the door shut. No noise.

"Ellie? Is that you?" Dad calls from the dining room. Apparently he has better hearing than Squash, our still-sleeping cat.

I step over the fat cat stretched out in the entryway. "Yeah, it's me!" I holler back, wishing it could be somebody else.

"Come in here! And hurry up!"

My dad couldn't know about the note yet. "Coming!" I grab my backpack with the note still inside. I brace myself.

Dad is sitting at the table. The table is so covered with papers, I can't even see the tablecloth. Paper wads decorate the floor.

"Dad? Are you all right?"

His hair looks like he stuck his head outside during a tornado. He glances up at me, and I notice the deep, dark circles under his eyes.

"I'm all right now that you're home, Ellie. What rhymes with *soap*?"

"Soap?" I repeat.

"No! You can't rhyme *soap* with *soap*!" he exclaims. "All I can think of is *dope*. And I'm not going to land the Riverfresh Soap account with that . . . although . . . hey, what do you think of this?

"Don't be a dope.
    Use Riverfresh Soap!"

Dad turns to me, eyes wide. He reminds me of Munch, Ethan's puppy. We picked Munch from the animal shelter partly because his big eyes made him look so cute. That was before he grew to the size of a colt. He's still growing.

"So? What do you think?" Dad demands.

I know my dad wants me to like his new jingle.

That's his job—coming up with great jingles and ads that get people to buy stuff.

Only this jingle isn't one of those great ones. "It . . . it sure does rhyme," I say, trying to let him down easy. "Totally rhymes."

Dad drops his pen. "It stinks, right? It's hopeless and silly and pointless. *I'm* hopeless. I've been at it all day. Tomorrow I have to present the company's jingle for a new soap campaign and whatnot. And I'm going to have nothing. Nada. Zero."

I take a seat across from my dad and brush aside the paper wads. "It's okay, Dad. You've still got *mope*, *rope*, *lope*. Personally, I love the word *lope*. It's a slow gallop, as smooth as a rocking horse."

I imagine riding a black stallion bareback as he lopes across an open pasture. . . .

"Ellie!" Dad calls me back. "Focus, honey. And no more horses. My boss says I've overdone the horse jingles. Think!"

"Hmm. There's always *hope*, Dad."

"Well, of course there's always hope," he says. "But I need a soap ad by tomorrow. And I can't have one if I don't have a lead jingle, now can I?"

"No. Dad, I mean *hope*."

"Right, right, right," he says, still not getting it. He sighs, resting his head on the table. "Mustn't lose hope and whatnot. You're right. Maybe there's something in *mope*?"

I reach across the table and put my hand on his. "Dad, how about this?

*"There's always hope
With Riverfresh Soap!"*

Dad's head boings up from the table. Lights flash through his eyeballs. "That's it! I can see it all now." He stands and paces. "A beautiful woman by a flowing river. Watching her from afar is a shy geek of a guy or whatnot. Should he? Could he? Dare he speak to this charming woman? Dare he try to meet her? He glances at the soap in his hand. Yes! Of course he should! Indeed he can! And why?" Dad smiles at me, and we say it together:

*"There's always hope
With Riverfresh Soap!"*

My dad is so excited about his new jingle that it just wouldn't be right to make him read the note from my teacher. Not now. He has work to do.

My little brother, Ethan, chooses this exact moment to dash into the house. From somewhere upstairs, Munch senses his master is home. Oversized paws thunder above us. The dog plows down the stairs. Munch gets a silent greeting from my brother.

Ethan and Munch barge into the dining room.

The dog skids on the hardwood floor. If I didn't know better, I'd think that dog has grown since this morning.

Ethan's hands fly in the air like birds gone wild as he signs to me, *Did you get in trouble for the note?*

I snap my fingers against my thumb fast a couple of times. In sign language that means, *No! No! No!*

Then behind me, I hear Dad. "What note?"

So much for hope. How am I going to dream my way out of this one?

4

Sorry

Ethan's fist goes to his heart and circles clockwise, the sign for *Sorry!*

He doesn't need to sign. His face says it all. He looks like he's been hit in the stomach with a fastball. My brother would never hurt anybody on purpose.

Before I can say anything, Dad moves in beside me and picks up my backpack. "Ellie, is there something in here I should know about? Like a note from your teacher?"

"Um . . . oh yeah. With the soap jingle and all,

I kind of forgot." I unzip the pocket of my pack.
"Maybe I should explain before–"

"No. That's quite all right. The note, please."
He stretches his arm out in jerks, like he's reaching
for a snake. The last time my parents had to come
in for a chat about my daydreaming, I overheard
Dad tell Mom that he felt like *he* was the kid who
had gotten into trouble.

I glance back at my brother. His fist is still
circling his heart.

Quickly, I sign back, *Not your fault.* Then I
hand Dad the note.

Ethan steps between Dad and me. If I'm the
smallest kid in fourth grade, my brother is the biggest in second. People ask us if we're twins.

Ethan grins at our dad and signs, *What are you
working on, Dad?*

Dad sets down the envelope so he can talk
and sign at the same time, which is what we all

do when Ethan is around, and sometimes when he's not. "We *were* working on a soap jingle and whatnot, Son. But now Ellie and I are going to have a little talk."

Now? Ethan signs. *I was hoping I could get a little help with my pitching.*

Ethan isn't making this up. Colt says Ethan has a great pitching arm, and Ethan is always looking for chances to practice.

Dad signs to Ethan, "I'd love to help you, Ethan. But I'm a little busy." He picks up the envelope again and waves it at us.

That's all right, Dad. I didn't mean you, Ethan signs.

"Ah. Right. Of course. But your mother's not home yet."

Mom played softball and basketball in college. Dad's the first to admit he's a klutz when it comes to sports.

How about Ellie? my loyal brother asks. *She can catch. And she's a good batter.*

Ethan knows I'm not a super player. Not like Colt. But I'm good enough that Brooks and Dylan come get me when they need another person on their team.

"I'm certain that your sister would be happy to help you bat and pitch and whatnot," Dad says and signs. "Unfortunately, Ellie and I need to—"

Dad's cell rings. He stares at it. Then he whispers to it, "Please don't be Ms. Warden."

Ms. Warden is Dad's boss at Jingle Bells Ad Agency. It's one of the biggest ad agencies in Kansas City. Colt's mom works there too. Sometimes she and my dad drive in to work together. But most of the time Mrs. Stevens goes in too early and stays too late.

Dad flips open his phone. He frowns, then puts the phone to his ear. "Hello, Ms. Warden?"

Ms. Warden's voice is so loud Dad has to hold the phone away from his ear. Mom says Dad's boss is "sassy as sand and older than dirt." But her lungs must be in good shape. Even I can hear her warning Dad to be prepared for the Riverfresh people.

Bang! Bang! Bang!

Somebody's pounding on the sliding door behind us. I look out to the backyard and see Colt. His nose is pressed to the glass. He looks like a cross between a fish and a pig—a fig. I almost laugh.

Colt holds up his catcher's mitt and motions Ethan and me outside.

I raise my eyebrows at Dad and let my eyes do the begging.

This makes me think about my science experiment. One of my three ways of trying to get a horse is supposed to be begging. I used to beg for a horse night and day until even I got tired of it.

It never got me anywhere. I suppose I could cross off begging already.

So that leaves crying and praying for a horse. Crying never worked. Plus, it made my eyes red. I gave up crying for a horse when I was about six.

So, God, that leaves You. I'll never stop praying for a horse. Praying isn't like begging or crying. I don't end up mad or sad. It just feels like God and I talk about the idea of me getting a horse. Most of the time I feel better after I pray about it, even though I'm pretty sure God keeps saying, *Not yet, Ellie.*

I begin imagining my dream black stallion. He prances up to take me away from all this trouble— from the dreaded note, from the conference with my parents, from Larissa the Fox Richland, who always finds the exact thing to say that will make me feel worse.

But Ethan interrupts. *Go!* He pushes me toward the door.

Dad is shooing us outside.

I can hear Dad's boss as the door shuts behind us.

"Thanks for the save, Colt," I say when we are safely outside. "Dad was just about to open the note when the phone rang."

Colt shrugs. "I'm just here because I promised to help Ethan with his pitching. That's all." He grins and tosses the ball to my brother.

"Yeah. I get it," I mutter. *Boys.*

Ethan fires the ball back to Colt.

"Nice!" Colt yells. With his glove on, it's tough to sign.

I love our backyard. Most yards in Hamilton are big enough to hold big dogs or pet pigs or just swing sets and stuff. Colt and I are lucky enough to be half in the country and half in town. Our backyards are bigger than ballparks.

Colt fires the ball to my brother. Then he

glances at me. "Who's your dad talking to? Miss Hernandez?"

I shake my head. "Ms. Warden." Now that I'm not worried about Dad yelling at me—for the moment—I wonder why Ms. Warden was yelling at Dad.

"Figures," Colt says. He and Ethan have a steady game of catch going. I like the regular *thwack, thwack* of the ball.

"What do you mean? Dad never gets calls from work when he's home." Mom says Dad leaves the office at the office.

"My mom gets calls at all hours. Woke me up last night. I couldn't get back to sleep." Colt holds the ball a few seconds too long, then turns to me. "Mom's pretty sure she's the one who's going to win the big promotion."

"Promotion? What promotion?"

Colt stares at me like *I've* turned into a

scroungy pinto. "You're kidding, right? *The* promotion."

When I show no clue of understanding, he
explains. "Jingle Bells Ad Agency needs a new
vice president. Everybody who works there is
trying to get that promotion. But your dad and
my mom are next in line for it. I can't believe your
dad hasn't told you about it."

"Dad was pretty freaked out over some soap
jingle thing. But he always gets that way when he
can't think of the right rhyme."

"Well, the promotion is all my mom talks
about. She really wants this job." Colt goes back
to playing catch with Ethan.

I glance in the sliding door. Dad is still on the
phone. Mostly he's listening.

Colt slips off his glove so he can sign to my
brother. "Great fastball. Need work on your curve."

Ethan nods.

There's a tap on the glass. Colt and I turn to look. Then Ethan follows our gaze. Dad crooks his finger at me to come in. Me. Just me.

I nod.

Ethan signs that he's praying for me. He means it. That kid prays about everything.

I touch my chin to sign, *Thanks*. I mean it too.

I leave Colt and Ethan and trudge in to face my dad.

"Hey, Dad. That was some phone call, huh? Everything okay at the office?" I grab a bottle of water and plop down at the table. I hope Dad will start telling me about the new promotion. I wouldn't mind at all if he forgot about my note.

"The office is fine," Dad says. "I had two phone calls, Ellie." He takes the chair next to mine. People say I look like my dad. I think they mean it as a good thing. He has big brown eyes and curly brown hair to match, like me. He's probably one of the shortest men at his work. Mom says he's "the best-lookin' dude this side of the Rockies."

"Two phone calls?" I'm thinking that gives us twice the chance of getting off the subject.

"Yes. Would you care to know who the second call was from?"

There's something fake calm in his voice. I'm pretty sure the real answer to this question is no. But I answer, "Sure, Dad."

"Principal Fishpaw."

My stomach twists. "Principal Fishpaw?"

"And do you know what he wanted?"

I shake my head no. But my stomach knows the answer is yes.

"He'd like us *all* to come in and talk about your daydreaming—again."

Most kids' dads would be shouting by now. Most dads would be angry if their kids got in trouble with the principal. But I know my dad is more scared than angry.

Fishpaw was Dad's principal when he went to school at Hamilton Elementary.

"Ellie," Dad goes on, "I thought you and I had a talk about your daydreaming at school."

"I know, Dad! But I wasn't daydreaming this time. Well, I was, but this was real. I mean, I wasn't daydreaming when I saw that horse out the window."

The front door opens and closes. Munch barks. Squash meows. Then my mom rushes in. The dog and cat are lost in the swirl of colors at Mom's feet. Her pink, orange, red, and blue peasant skirt balloons over her purple sandals. My mom refuses to own a single white, gray, or black piece of clothing. She tries to mix as many colors as she can on a given day. "If it's good enough for rainbows," she says when somebody claims her colors clash, "it's good enough for me."

"I'm as tired as a two-pound hen with a three-pound egg. What a day!" Mom kisses Dad and me on the tops of our heads. She could do this even if we were standing. She's very tall. And we're very not. In Mom's own words, she's so tall that if she fell down anywhere, she'd be halfway home.

"Rough day, Bev?" Dad asks.

My mom is a professional volunteer. She helps out at a different place every day. I'm pretty sure today was cat farm day. Mom pets stray and half-wild cats so they get tame enough to be adopted.

Mom plops into a chair. She slides down so that her legs sprawl all the way under the table. Her short black hair is sweat-glued to her forehead. "Well, let's see," she begins. "How *was* my day? I guess it was fine . . . right up to the part where I lost a horse."

5

Lost

"Mom, did you say you lost a horse?" My mind is racing. *A horse?* My mother lost a horse?

"How could you lose a horse, Bev?" Dad asks.

"Well, it wasn't all that hard," Mom says as if she's about to explain how she lost a game of Go Fish. She scratches Munch. The giant dog lays his head in my mom's lap.

"I was on my way to the cat farm," she begins. "Then I remembered I'd promised to stop by the skilled nursing care center. I do love volunteering there—you know how much I love the elderly. But this morning, Mrs. Sanders insisted on planting violets. I said I'd be happy to do it for her. But *no*, she had to do it herself—with my help, of course. Now, it's no secret that Mrs. Sanders is a couple of sandwiches shy of a picnic. But let me tell you, that woman has more energy in her little finger than any two people combined."

Mom has said all of this without taking a breath. Colt says my mother could get into *Guinness World Records* for longest talking without breath taking.

Mom inhales and continues. "But that was nothing. Off to the cat farm I went. And the minute I arrived, things went completely catawampus! Mary Louise was in a tizzy because someone had called to say they were dropping off a new rescue. I thought it a bit odd because people generally don't announce when they're ditching their cats. We've taken on a dozen cats at once before, so I didn't understand why Mary Louise was so bothered by a single drop-off rescue cat. Except that the woman—and I love her to death, you know I do—can have a cow over breaking her fingernail. So of course I told her not to give it another thought. I'd be happy to handle the new rescue by myself."

I'm dying for her to get to the part about losing a horse. But you can't hurry my mom. Believe me. I've tried.

She takes another breath. "I found an old crate in the barn and made a fine bed for the newcomer as far away from the other cats as I could. Well, I was just about finished when I heard Mary Louise holler, 'Land o' livin'! Bev! You'd best come out here and see for yourself!' So I did just that. And what do you think I saw?"

"A horse?" I ask, hoping we're finally getting to the good part.

Mom shakes her head and takes in a giant

breath. "A long black trailer, that's what! 'Why would they waste a trailer on a cat?' I asked nobody in particular because Mary Louise had disappeared. I admit the thought occurred to me that *cat* might also mean lion, tiger, and the like. So it was with great caution that I made my way to that trailer."

"And . . . ?" I urge.

"Don't tell me—!" Dad says.

"*Do* tell *me*!" I beg.

Mom looks from Dad to me and back before she goes on. "Well, I got up all my courage. I walked to the trailer and peered in. And what do you think I saw?"

"A horse?" I cry.

"A horse!" Mom exclaims. "I'll be an ant's aunt if I didn't!"

I can't believe this. I've helped Mom at the cat farm before. There's a barn there, and I guess it has stalls. But the whole barn is filled with cats.

Mom takes in a deep breath and turns to me. "I wish you had been there, Ellie. You know I'm as useless as a trapdoor in a canoe when it comes to horses. But the driver of the trailer unlocked the tailgate and told me the horse was all mine. Then he just disappeared."

"What did you do?" I press.

"I put down the tailgate and walked into the trailer. That poor old horse seemed half dead, tied up so tight it couldn't move. So I untied it. I told it to stay put while I cleared the cats out of one of the stalls. And that's exactly what I did. I went to the barn and chased the cats out of the corner stall. Only when I went back to the trailer . . ."

"The horse was gone!" I shout because I can't stand it another minute. "Mom, did that horse have black-and-white spots?"

"Why, yes. It *was* spotted. I can't say, though,

if it was black with white spots or white with black spots."

"And did it look like it hadn't had a good meal in a long time?" I ask.

Mom looks amazed. "Oh, my, yes. That poor creature would have to stand up twice to leave a shadow." She stops talking and stares at me. "Ellie, how on earth did you know that horse was skinny and spotted?"

"Because you lost the horse I imagined! Mom, I found your horse!"

6

Coincidence?

Dad and I do our best to bring Mom up to speed on my "imaginary" horse and Dad's call from Principal Fishpaw. Then Ethan comes in. And we have to explain all over again.

"Well, if that don't beat the band, as your granny used to say!" Mom exclaims.

"Some coincidence, all right," Dad agrees.

I grin at Ethan. I know what he's thinking. Ethan says there's no such thing as a coincidence. Only God-things—events only God could bring together.

I have to agree with my brother on this one.

My seeing the same spotted horse Mom lost? Definitely a God-thing. "So wait a minute. Where's the horse now?"

"I have no idea," Mom answers.

"Are you saying the horse is still out there? She's not still lost, is she?"

"Mary Louise has the entire Hamilton police force out searching," Mom says.

"Mom, the entire police force means Sheriff Duffy and his deputy, right? And Sheriff Duffy is scared to death of horses. Not to mention cows and sheep."

"True," Mom admits. "That sheriff is pretty much all hat and no cattle." She yawns, stretching her long arms and knocking the plaque with our family crest off the wall. She picks it up with a broad sweep of her arm. "Mary Louise said if they had any trouble, she'd call the animal control people to come help."

"No!" I cry. "You can't let animal control get to that horse! You know what they do to homeless animals!"

I know what they do to them. They "put them to sleep."

"I didn't think of that," Mom admits. She grabs her keys off the table. "You're right. I lost that horse. And it's up to me to find it. It's my civic duty." She aims a half smile at my dad, who is used to her civic duty. "There's meat loaf in the fridge, Lenny."

"Bev, do you have to go?" Dad begs. "Can't they get along without you for once?"

Mom shakes her head. "I feel responsible. I've never lost a horse before."

Dad frowns at the papers scattered across the table. Then he scoots his chair back and stands tall. If my dad had two heads, one on top of the other, he'd be almost as tall as my mom. "I'm coming with you. You're going to need help."

Mom leans over—and down—to kiss Dad's cheek. "You are one sweet man, Lenny James. But a cowboy you are not."

That's saying it nicely. I've never seen my dad on a horse. As the story goes, he only rode once, when he was a toddler. I guess he fell off and landed on his head.

I take Mom's hand. "Come on, Mom! We have to find that spotted horse before the animal control guys do."

Mom doesn't argue. She knows I'm her only chance of rescuing that rescue horse.

We jump into the car, and Mom heads toward Main Street. Gravel crunches under our wheels. After two blocks, Mom turns onto Main Street. It's the only street that goes through town. She drives past the library, the bank, and the hardware store and up to the only stoplight. It blinks red instead of changing colors. She stops for half a second, then goes again.

"Maybe we should check out by the cemetery," I suggest. "People would have noticed a horse on Main Street."

Mom spins a U-turn, hangs a left, and drives toward the cemetery.

"What if they already caught the mare?" I ask, bouncing with the bumpy road.

"Mary Louise promised to call me if they did," Mom says. "And I haven't heard from her yet."

I scan each cross street we pass. When the gravel turns to dirt, I look for hoofprints. But I don't see any.

Mom drives out of town a couple of miles in each direction. Usually I gaze out the window and imagine riding my black show horse over the green Missouri hills. But right now I'm too busy searching for a runaway horse.

Mom's cell phone rings.

"I'll get it." I'm scared to death it's going to be Mary Louise telling us the animal control people have the horse.

The cell is in the bottom of Mom's huge purse. The ringtone is almost over—an Elvis song that makes me want to fling the whole purse out the window—when I finally get to it. "Hello?"

"Ellie?" The caller sounds confused. I think it's Colt.

"Colt?" I'm the only kid on the planet who doesn't have a cell phone. So Colt calls Mom's if he thinks I'm with her.

"Yeah. It's Colt."

"I can't talk now. Mom and I are trying to find a lost horse before—"

"I know!" he shouts. "I called your house to tell you. Your dad said to call the cell. They found it!"

"What?"

"The horse! They found the horse," Colt says.

"Where? Is she all right?"

The phone crackles. I turn to Mom. "Hurry! Head back to town." Then I scream into the phone, "Colt? Where's the horse?"

Colt's voice mixes with the crackles of the phone. "At school! And you'd better get here fast. I have a feeling this old nag is running out of time."

7

The Chase

"Hurry, Mom!" I grip the dashboard as Mom wheels back to town.

"Sorry, Ellie," Mom says. "I can't afford to get another speeding ticket."

"But what if we're too late? What if the animal control guys get there first? What if–?"

"Stop what-iffing. Your engine's in overdrive and nobody's driving."

I'm not sure I get that one. I try to stop imagining what might be happening at the school right now. Only I can't stop.

The muddy, spotted horse staggers across the school lawn. She wobbles in the fading sunlight, dazed, sides heaving. Four animal control guys dressed in white stand in the corners of the yard and hurl a net into the air. It crashes down on the poor horse, knocking her to the ground.

A guy from animal control smirks at the crowd. His face is scarred. His eyes are glowing beads of fire. "What say ye?" he asks the crazed crowd.

A hundred fists rise. A hundred thumbs turn down. "Death to the nag!" they cry.

The people in white yank the net. It closes on the horse. They drag her off to their cage on wheels and . . .

Thankfully, Mom slams the brakes, stopping the car and my imagination.

"Will you look at that crowd!" Mom exclaims.

I gaze out my window at all the people in the streets, in the school yard, everywhere.

Mom leans on the steering wheel. "Surely they can't all be here for that little horse."

I hurry out of the car. Not only are the animal control people here, but the town's two police cars are parked on the school lawn. Orange cones block off the roads in all directions. Even the fire truck is here.

It looks like half the town found the horse before we did.

I spot Colt up the street and run to meet him.

"Ellie!" he shouts, waving both arms like he's directing traffic.

Larissa is with him. She doesn't wave. Not even with one arm.

"Cool, huh?" Colt says when we meet up in the center of the street.

"What are these people all doing here?

Where's the horse? What's going on?" For the millionth time, I wish I were taller. I can't see over the heads in the crowd.

"It's been awesome!" Colt exclaims. "Nobody can catch that skinny horse."

Larissa takes a sip from a long, curly straw poked into her pink drink. The giant plastic cup says Crazy Larry's Dairies. "All this fuss over a backyard horse?" She says this without bothering to look up from her Crazy Larry's cup.

"Backyard horse?" I repeat.

Larissa sighs. "That's what my mother calls them. Backyard horses. You know. A horse without papers. Not registered. Probably not even a purebred. The kind of nag somebody would keep in the backyard instead of paying to board it in a stable."

I stare at her and wonder why God gave Larissa Richland a champion show horse. *Her* horse has probably never even seen Larissa's backyard. Custer's Darling Delight (great horse, silly name) goes directly from the elite K. C. Stables to the horse show ring and back again.

I start to argue with her, then stop. "I don't have time for this."

Suddenly the crowd lets out an "Oooh–aah!"

Larissa, Colt, and I spin around to see.

"There it goes again!" Colt laughs.

"What?" I stand on tiptoes and try to see. But I'm too short. Too many heads are in the way. "What's happening?"

"That horse just dodged a net," Colt explains.

"A net?" It's like I imagined. This is not good. "I have to see what's going on." I leave Colt and Larissa and take off running for the horse.

"You're not supposed to go up there!" Larissa calls after me. "You're going to get in trouble. Anyway, it's just a backyard nag, Ellie."

I ignore her and her singsong threat. Just

because *her* horse wins trophies all over the state doesn't give her the right to make fun of other horses. But she does it all the time. My friend Rashawn has a sweet gray farm horse named Dusty. Larissa calls him Musty or Rusty and laughs about it every time, like she's so funny. Rashawn's best friend, Cassandra, has a Shetland pony, and Larissa is always making fun of him too. She calls him Phony Pony.

I elbow my way through the crowd. "Excuse me, please!"

"Watch where you're going, kid!"

I glance up to see a guy in a baseball cap that says *Channel 5 News*. He has a video camera strapped to one hand. Two more cameras dangle around his neck.

Next to him, six middle school girls are snapping photos with their cells.

Finally I break through the pack. Somebody

behind me gasps. I look up in time to see the spotted horse trot right in front of us. It's the first good look I've gotten of the horse. I hate to admit it, but if Larissa ever had the right to make fun of a horse, this would be the one.

If anything, the mare is dirtier than when I saw her the first time. And skinnier. I could count her ribs from here. Her backbone sticks up so far she looks swayback, although I don't think she is. What mane she has is knotted into tangles of burs and sticks. Her dingy black-and-white tail looks shorter than Miss Hernandez's ponytail.

The horse takes off again, tearing chunks out of the school lawn with her hooves. People scatter out of the way. I spot Principal Fishpaw. His face is as red as Larissa's hair. I'm not sure if he's screaming at the pinto or at everybody else.

On the other side of the lawn, Sheriff Duffy waves his cowboy hat at the horse and shouts,

"Shoo!" When the pinto keeps trotting toward him, the sheriff explodes at his deputy. "Get her, Jeremy!" Then he dashes behind a tree. If Sheriff Duffy thinks he's hiding behind the tree, he's wrong. His belly sticks out on both sides.

I need to get closer to the horse. But I don't want to scare her. She's had enough of humans. I dash to the maple tree I observe every day from my classroom. Pressed against the rough bark, I can hear the pinto's breath coming in snorts. The sound seems to be getting closer with each breath.

Carefully, I peek around the tree for a better look.

The pinto is so close I could touch her spots if I had longer arms. She's definitely spotted black and white under all that mud. One spot on her back really is shaped like a saddle. Without measuring her, I can't tell if she's over 14.2 hands, which would make her a horse instead of a pony.

Her neck looks long, but it might be because it's so skinny. And that might be why her ears look too big for her head.

All in all, this horse is not much to look at. But she sure can run.

"Chase her this way!" a tall man in a white uniform shouts from the other side of the lawn. This guy I recognize. Mr. Yanke from animal control.

About a year ago he captured Squash, our cat. And Squash wasn't even lost. He'd just wandered off to explore. He would have come home if Mr. Yanke had left him alone. We had to fight—and pay fifty dollars—to get our own cat back.

Mr. Yanke has something in his hands. Sunlight gleams off the object when he lifts it and points it at the pinto.

I have to find out what he's holding and what he's planning to do with it. I shoot off a prayer. Then I step from my hiding place and jog over to him.

I've almost made it when, from the far end of the lawn, I hear, "Yee-haw!"

I spin around to see the other person from animal control, Yanke's partner. She's waving her arms and running behind the pinto.

The poor horse lunges left. But Sheriff Duffy is there, screaming. With a screech like that, he could star in a horror movie.

The horse breaks right. But the deputy is there. Then the animal control lady, the sheriff, and his deputy join forces to chase the pinto up the lawn . . . and straight toward Mr. Yanke.

I can still see that silver thing in his hand.

"Ellie!" Mom comes running up. "I've been searching all over for you, and—" She gasps. "Oh no. He's not going to—"

"Mom, what? What's he going to do?"

"That thing in his hand," she whispers. "I think it's a stun gun."

8

Caught

I know what a stun gun is. I've seen it on TV. Policemen use it to shock bad guys. That thing can zap even a big man off his feet.

But this pinto isn't a bad guy. She didn't do anything wrong. The only reason she's running away is because everybody's chasing her.

With the sheriff, the deputy, and the animal control lady coming after her, the pinto breaks into an unsteady gallop. She's getting closer and closer to me . . . and to Yanke, who is ready with his stun gun. The siren on the fire truck goes off.

People are shouting. It's a disaster movie. The only thing missing is a sky filled with helicopters to film the big event.

That's it!

"Mr. Yanke!" I leap in front of him and point to the sky. "Are those helicopters? Are they filming us?"

Mr. Yanke's eyes grow big. He lowers his stun gun and straightens his cap. Then he peers up at the sky . . . just as the pinto races past us. "I don't see any helicopters."

"Really?" I take a step back. "Huh. Guess I'm seeing things."

Sheriff Duffy is the first to reach us. He glares at Yanke. "What happened? You let that nag run right past you!"

The deputy is behind him. "Yeah! We had him right where we wanted him!"

"Her," I correct.

The three of them frown at me.

Yanke's partner storms up to him. She whips off her cap and smacks it against her thigh. "What gives? You could have reached out and stunned that creature and been done with this whole circus!"

Mr. Yanke jumps in. "Well, I *was* going to stun her. Then this kid . . ." He glares at me.

I smile back at them. "He's right. Mr. Yanke was totally ready to stun that horse all by himself."

Mr. Yanke gives them an I-told-you-so nod and waits for me to finish.

"That's because . . . how did you put it, Mr. Yanke? Everybody else here is too chicken-livered scared to help?"

"Hey!" the sheriff cries. "*I* wasn't scared."

"Me neither!" his deputy claims.

"*You're* the one who hates horses," Yanke's partner mutters.

"*Me?*" Yanke shouts. "What about *you?*"

I leave them outshouting each other while I sneak off to find the pinto.

The crowd has thinned. It's starting to get dark, and I've lost sight of the horse. Then I see her by the flag pole. I move in closer and can see every muscle of the horse's skinny back quivering. She looks ready to fly out of there the second she senses danger.

I'm no danger. I just have to convince her of that. "Hey, girl," I say in a cheery voice as I inch closer to her.

Behind me, I hear Colt's voice. "Stand back, people! Give Ellie a chance. She's good with horses."

I'm grateful to Colt for holding back the crowd.

"So," I tell the pinto, "you've had quite a day. Me too. Don't get me started. First I see you, but nobody believes me. Then–"

I keep a steady stream of babble going. Inside, I'm praying, although I'm not even sure what I'm saying—inside or out. I figure God understands anyway.

I carefully inch toward the mare. "Who likes to be chased, right?"

She sidesteps.

"Whoa, now."

She takes a few steps backward. I go with her. I stop, and she stops.

Now what?

I keep talking. "Sure glad we found you, Ms. Pinto. My mom's really sorry she lost you. She loses things a lot. But you're the first horse she's lost."

The chatter isn't working anymore. I can see the muscles in the pinto's shoulders knot. She's thinking about bolting. I don't know what to do to stop her. She'll run away. She'll be lost again.

Before I realize what I'm doing, I hear myself singing:

"I once was lost but now am found
  Was blind but now I see.
  Amazing grace! How sweet
    the sound . . ."

The pinto's big, fuzzy ears prick up. I keep singing, even though Granny used to say I couldn't carry a tune in a bucket with the lid on. I take a step toward the horse, and she doesn't move away.

I've watched Mr. Harper catch the horses he lets us ride in horsemanship practice. And I've noticed a funny thing about those horses. They play hard to get. If Mr. Harper walks into a pasture full of horses, the only one that runs from him is the one he wants. I've always wondered what would happen if he pretended he was there for a different horse.

It's worth a try now. This pinto sure has been playing hard to get.

I keep singing as I walk closer to her. But I look past her, off to the side, like I'm going for a different horse—not her. I get so close I feel the heat of her sweaty neck.

Slowly, without looking at her, I reach up and scratch under her neck. She lets me. I ease my hand up toward her mane.

With my arm draped around the horse, I start singing again. This time I sing my own words to the tune of "Amazing Grace":

"I need a rope for this spotted horse.
     Won't somebody slip me a rope?
     'Cause if you don't,
     This horse will lope.
     And will I catch her? Nope!"

I keep singing, glad that—thanks to Dad's soap jingle—I know so many words that rhyme with *rope*.

"She should stop singing," Larissa complains. "That's not how the song goes."

But Colt gets it. He disappears for a minute. When he comes running back, he's carrying a rope behind his back. I don't know where he found it, and I don't ask. He slips it to me. I loop it around the pinto's neck and pull the end through, and I've got myself a lead rope.

I take a step, and so does the pinto. The way she's panting, I'm not too worried about her running off on me now.

Mr. Yanke comes jogging up to us. I wish he wouldn't. I can feel the pinto tense up at the sight of him.

"All right then," he says. "You, uh . . . you shouldn't stand so close to that horse, girl. Don't know what you were thinking. I'll take it from here." He reaches for my rope.

"I don't think so," I say.

"Well, maybe it wouldn't hurt for you to take her on up into my trailer." The pinto swishes her tail. Mr. Yanke jumps back.

"Still don't think so," I tell him. "I'm taking her back to the . . ." I stop myself before I mention the cat farm. "To the animal farm."

"The what?" he asks.

"Well done, Ellie!" Mom comes running up. She's barefoot, carrying her sandals. "I wish your father could have seen that." She narrows her eyes at Mr. Yanke. "Can we help you?"

"I told your girl here that she could put that horse in my trailer. Or she could hand it over to me now."

"And I told Mr. Yanke that I was taking the pinto back to the *animal* farm." I wink at Mom and pray she takes the cue.

"What's she talking about?" he asks. "Does

she mean that cat farm north of town? They don't have horses out there."

Mom grins at him. "They do now."

9

Journey

Mom stands side by side with me and the pinto as Mr. Yanke storms off to his empty horse trailer.

Behind us, I hear clapping. Wild applause bursts out across the school yard.

I look around to see what everybody's clapping about.

"Take a bow, Ellie!" Colt shouts.

"Me?" They're clapping for me? I see our mailman, Mr. Blackburn. And my first-grade teacher, Miss Tomlin. And two high school girls, cheerleaders for the Hamilton Hornets. They're all clapping for *me*.

The pinto starts dancing around. She doesn't like the noise. With only the rope around her neck, I don't think I could hold her if she took off on me.

Somebody tosses me a halter. I reach out and catch it.

"It's an extra I had in the truck!" Mr. Harper says.

"Thanks, Mr. Harper!" I call back. Sometimes people turn out to be even nicer than I thought they were.

From somewhere in the thinning crowd, Larissa's whine comes through. "Big deal. So she caught an ugly backyard horse."

And sometimes people aren't nicer than I thought.

I slip on the halter and buckle it. It's a little big, but it should do the trick. Then I fasten the rope.

"I'll lead her to the cat farm," I tell Mom.

"Honey, it must be two miles to that barn." She glances at Mr. Yanke's trailer. "Maybe we could–"

"No way, Mom! It's safer if I walk her. Okay?"

Mom sighs. "All right. I'll call your father and let him know we'll be late."

We set out at a slow pace, taking the back roads. The sun's dropped out of sight, but I can see all right. Once I let the pinto graze along the roadside. But she takes only one bite of clover. Then she jerks her head up and snorts, like she expects somebody to take it away from her. No wonder she's so skinny. Who owned her before she ended up here? I'd like to know what they did to make her so skittish.

I sing to her for most of the journey. Whenever I stop, she prances sideways and begins trembling again. So I run through every song I can think of. Colt would be rolling in the ditch laughing if he were here. He says Ethan is lucky because he can't hear me sing.

It takes us an hour to get to the cat farm. The whole time Mom follows me in her car. I didn't know cars could go that slow. But I'm thankful for the headlights because by the time I get to the barn, it's pitch dark. I'm not sure who's more tired—the pinto, Mom, or me.

"There's a tank of water in the corner stall," Mom says. She goes into the barn first and pulls a string that turns on an overhead light. Shadows streak the barn floor.

We shoo cats out of the stall. The pinto walks straight in and starts drinking. I watch her long, skinny neck stretch to the water tank and gulp, gulp, gulp.

"You're really thirsty, aren't you, girl?" I stroke the soft underside of her neck and feel the water swoosh down.

I unhook the lead rope but leave her halter on so she won't be so hard to catch.

Together Mom and I drag down a bale of hay from the loft. Then we cover the stall floor with a layer of straw. It's not easy because a million cats swarm around our feet while we work. It's a miracle the pinto doesn't step on any of them.

A scrawny calico cat jumps onto the pinto's back and curls up there, purring. Spots on spots. I expect the mare to buck her off, but she doesn't.

"Let's go home, Ellie," Mom says. "I'm dead on my feet and running on empty."

I latch the stall door behind me and take one last look at the horse. I sure hope somebody can get those burs out of her mane and tail. She needs a good brushing too.

We trudge to the car and head home. Outside my car window the moon looks like someone took a bite out of it. "What's going to happen to her?" I ask.

"I'll make some calls tomorrow," Mom says,

yawning behind the wheel. "We'll find somewhere that can take her. She'll be fine."

I nod. But I can't help thinking that horse hasn't been fine for a long time—maybe ever.

At home, Ethan and Dad make us give them a blow-by-blow description of the great horse rescue. By the time I crawl into bed, it's really late.

I say my prayers anyway, like I do every night. I know I need to talk to God more during the day. But I forget. Sometimes a whole day goes by and I haven't even said hey to God. So at least I make sure to check in at night.

That was really something today, God. Thanks for helping me catch that pinto. Please take care of her from now on. Find somebody to comb out that mane of hers. And brush her. And trim her hooves. And fatten her up.

It's hard to get the picture of the pinto out of my mind. Just before we left, she turned her neck and looked right at me. Then she nickered. It was a soft rumble that sounded like a thank-you.

After I pray for Mom and Dad and Ethan and everybody, I do what I've done every night for the past six or seven years. I ask God to give me a beautiful black stallion, a show horse that could win the Hamilton Royal Horse Show.

My bedroom window opens onto our back-yard. Sometimes at night after I finish praying for a horse, I imagine one coming to visit me. Tonight I picture myself opening my window and a black stallion cantering up and sticking his head in so I can pet him and kiss his soft muzzle.

As I drift off to sleep, I can almost hear him nicker.

10

Worry

"I don't see why we have to go through with this parent-teacher-principal meeting now that everybody in town knows Ellie really did see a spotted horse from her classroom," Dad says. Mom is driving us to school for the dreaded meeting. Ethan is along for the ride.

"I agree with Dad," I say helpfully.

"Ellie," Mom says, glancing into the rearview mirror for eye contact, "what did your teacher say when you asked her about the meeting?"

"She said Principal Fishpaw still wants to talk with us," I mumble.

"Exactly," she says.

"Well," Dad complains, "it makes a rotten ending to a perfect day."

"You had a perfect day?" I ask. My day wasn't perfect—not even close. A few kids congratulated me on catching the "ugly horse." But even more people teased me about it. Plus, I forgot to write up my plan for the science experiment. So I'm already down five points.

"Yes. A perfect day," Dad repeats. "Thanks to you, Ellie."

"Me?"

"You gave me *hope*."

Then I remember. "Your jingle! Did the soap people like it?"

"They loved it! We got the account." Dad

smiles at me from the front seat. "Couldn't have done it without your rhyme."

"Way to go, Dad!"

Ethan taps Dad's shoulder and signs, *Congratulations!*

"I knew you'd pull it off, Lenny," Mom says. "That must have gone down finer than frog's hair with your boss."

"I believe Ms. Warden was as happy as I've ever seen her," Dad says. "The corners of her mouth turned up for a full three seconds. Moira Stevens, on the other hand, stormed out of the board room without a word. Quite surprising."

After what Colt told me about how much his mother wants that promotion, I'm not surprised at all.

"I hardly see Moira anymore," Mom says. She turns in to the school parking lot. "We chat on the phone sometimes. But all she talks about is that promotion. Does she realize she'll have to be away from her family for weeks at a time if she gets that job?"

Dad shrugs. "Speaking of being away, what's up with Jeff Stevens? I haven't seen Jeff around for weeks. I know he travels and whatnot . . ." Dad lowers his voice and stops signing, which makes me think something's up at Colt's house.

Part of me wants to pray that Colt's mom doesn't get that promotion. Part of me wants to pray that my dad doesn't get it either. I'd hate for him to be gone all the time.

And this is one of the confusing things about praying. What if I'm praying my dad won't get the promotion, but he's praying he will?

I ask God to watch out for Colt. I'll let God figure out the rest.

Dad tries to talk Mom out of the meeting at

school right up to the second we knock on the principal's office door.

"Maybe I should wait here with Ethan?" he suggests.

Ethan has already claimed the only folding chair in the hallway. He's lost in his graphic novel.

"You're being silly, Lenny," Mom says, knocking again.

The door cracks open. My principal sticks out his head. He frowns at us like he suspects we're secretly here to rob the place.

Finally he swings the door wide open and motions us to his inner office. No one goes to the Fishpaw inner office unless they're in serious trouble. Three kids went in and never came out. At least that's what Colt's big sister, Sierra, told us.

We follow Principal Fishpaw single file. He towers over all of us, except Mom. I reach back and take hold of Dad's hand. But it's too sweaty, so I let go again. I don't think Dad notices.

My teacher greets us and shakes Mom's and Dad's hands. I catch her wiping her hand on her blue-and-white sweatpants after she shakes Dad's hand.

"Thank you so much for coming." Miss Hernandez points to the three small chairs across the desk from the principal's king-sized chair. "Please take a seat." She leans against the edge of the desk, and my principal takes his throne.

As usual, Principal Fishpaw is wearing a suit, socks, and sandals. Sometimes in the winter he wears shoes with no socks. It's a mystery. He's about twice the size of my dad. His head makes me think of our lawn—with tufts of grass in odd places.

Principal Fishpaw fixes his gaze on my dad. "Leonard, it's good to see you here again."

Leonard? Nobody calls Dad Leonard. He's just Lenny or Dad.

Dad doesn't correct the principal. "Thank you, sir," he says.

"Brings back memories, doesn't it?" my principal asks. "You and me sitting across this very desk after I called you to the principal's office?"

Sweat forms in tiny balls across Dad's forehead. "Well, that was a long time ago–"

"Not so long ago!" Principal Fishpaw bellows, as if my dad is trying to pick a fight with him.

Dad tries to grin, but he looks like he has a stomachache. "Yes. Well, I-I-I guess we should have called off this meeting."

"Called off the meeting?" Principal Fishpaw roars. "Why on earth would I do such a thing?"

Dad grips the seat of his chair as if Principal Fishpaw's roar might blow him out of the office. "I mean . . . you know . . . since Ellie did see the horse and whatnot?"

Miss Hernandez smiles at me. "I owe you an

apology, Ellie. When you shouted in class that you saw a horse, I admit I thought it was your imagination talking."

"Wait a minute." Principal Fishpaw glares at my dad. "What do you mean, your daughter saw a horse from her classroom? Were you there, Leonard? In that classroom? Have you decided to repeat fourth grade?"

Dad clears his throat. "Well, no. Of course not. I have a job. A very good job."

"So what you're telling me is that you weren't there. You didn't see any horses from the fourth-grade window, did you? You have no way of knowing if Ellie saw that imaginary horse."

"Well," Dad stammers, "wh-when you put it like that . . ."

"Dwayne!" Mom snaps.

Dad, Miss Hernandez, and I turn to Mom. But she has locked her glare onto my principal.

"Yes, Bev?" Principal Fishpaw answers.

My mom never had Mr. Fishpaw as a principal because she didn't grow up here. But she knows everybody in Hamilton. She's on the school board and president of the Parent-Teacher Organization.

"Dwayne Fishpaw—" Mom slaps the desk, and we jump—"it's high time to use the sense the good Lord gave you, hear? Not only did *Ellie* see the horse, but *I* saw this 'imaginary' horse with my own two eyes. Now, are you going to quit bullying my husband and apologize to my daughter or not?"

✷ ✷ ✷

"You were wonderful, Bev!" Dad exclaims for the tenth time as we pile into the car.

"Nonsense," Mom says. "That man would start an argument with a grapefruit."

11

Teamwork

While Dad continues to rave about Mom's bravery and his great blessing in finding a wife like her, I give Ethan an update in sign.

We drive through Crazy Larry's and get ice cream to celebrate. Then we head for the cat farm to check on the pinto.

At the barn, Ethan, Mom, and I climb out of the car. "Careful not to step on cats," Mom warns.

Dad stays put. "I'll be along as soon as I finish my fudge sundae," he promises.

The minute we step into the barn, a dozen cats

scatter. Then I hear it—that nicker. I glance back at Ethan and realize he can't hear it. And for one of the few times ever, I feel sorry for my brother. This is one sound I can't begin to describe to him.

Ethan helps me pull down a bale of hay, even though I'm not sure the pinto touched what we left last night. I try to get her to eat out of my hand. She nibbles at it but doesn't seem hungry.

When Dad comes in, I think we're going to leave. But he takes one look at the pinto and says, "Is that horse sick? She's so skinny."

I check the pinto's eyes and hooves. She doesn't look sick. I wish she could tell us what's wrong.

"Mary Louise had the vet out this morning, just to make sure the horse is okay before we send her off again," Mom reports. "He gave her a clean bill of health. Only thing wrong with her is that she needs to put on weight."

"We should try feeding her oats," I suggest. I slip into the stall with her. "I bet she'd go for Omolene."

"What's that?" Dad asks.

"It's like oats, but with bran and flax and oils. Smells like molasses. We learned about it in 4-H. I thought it smelled good enough to eat."

"Why don't I go get some?" Dad says.

"Really?" I'm surprised. I didn't think he liked horses.

"It's the least I can do for that poor horse," he answers. "I'm pretty sure the farmer's supply stays open until nine."

Dad leaves, and the rest of us conduct a barn search for brushes. Ethan finds an old horse brush and hands it to me. I set to work. Dust flies off the mare with every stroke of the brush. I use my fingernails to loosen some of the mud clumps.

Meanwhile, Mom tackles the horse's tangled

mane and tail. She uses her own comb on some of the burs.

Ethan unties the lead rope I attached to the feed trough so the pinto wouldn't move around while we brushed her.

"What are you doing?" I ask him, shoving the brush under my arm so I can sign.

Ethan doesn't answer. Instead, he begins retying the rope.

"Ethan?" I demand.

He points at me and signs, *Overhand knot. Bad.* He ties the rope like I had it and shakes his head. He's probably right, but it's the only knot I know.

Square knot, Ethan signs. Then he makes a knot that really does look like a square.

He unties the square knot and whips the rope into a knot shaped like a cursive capital *S. Half hitch*, he signs. *I'll teach you that one later.*

I watch as my little brother unties the half

hitch and starts over. This time he makes two loops with the rope, twists them twice, then feeds the lead rope through a hook at the end of the trough. When he jerks the rope, it doesn't slip. It's tied tight. *Cat's-paw,* he signs.

Nothing my brother does surprises me. I give him a thumbs-up and go back to brushing.

I reach the funny saddle-shaped spot on the pinto's back. I brush the hairs backward to get at the dust, then smooth down the coat. "Mom? I've been thinking."

"Mm-hmm?"

I move down the mare's foreleg. "What if, instead of sending the horse away, you guys kept her here?"

"Here? You'd be putting a toad in a teakettle, kiddo." Mom laughs a little. "Honey, this is a *cat* farm. Mary Louise doesn't like horses. She's terrified a horse might accidently step on one of the kittens."

What's going to happen to her? Ethan signs.

Mom stops combing the pinto's mane. "We've been making calls. Nothing's settled yet. I guess the last place only had the horse for three days before sending her to us. They don't want her back."

They won't send her to animal control, will they? Ethan asks.

The idea makes my stomach and heart flip over and trade places.

"No. Of course not," Mom answers.

But Mom doesn't run the cat farm.

We brush and comb in silence until Dad gets back with the feed. Right away the pinto noses the Omolene.

"Well, look at you!" Dad exclaims when she actually nibbles the grain. He looks as proud as if he has baked it himself.

We walk to the car in moonlight. It's quiet

except for a howl that could be a coyote. We have a few out in the country around here.

I glance back at the pinto. Her face is lit by the single light bulb we've kept on in the barn for her. She's watching us leave, her head leaning out over the stall door. But she doesn't nicker. I can't help wondering if she knows she won't be staying here long. Maybe she figures we're not ever coming back.

I'm bone tired when I climb into bed. But it takes me a long time to fall asleep. I ask God to find a good home for the pinto.

Before long, my thoughts turn to the Hamilton Royal Horse Show. All year I wait for it. Now it's only a week away. And each year I pray that next time I'll have a horse of my own to ride in the show.

But here we are again, and still no horse.

Dear God, I pray as I drift off to sleep, *there's a lot about praying that I don't understand. I know You can do anything. So how come You haven't done this? Please, by this time next year, will You let me have my own horse to ride in the show? And thanks for not getting tired of me asking. I've given up crying and begging my parents. So You're all I've got. I know You're all I need. It's just that it's getting harder to keep praying for a horse that never comes.*

Right before I fall asleep, I gaze out the window and imagine my prizewinning black stallion galloping in the moonlight.

Only this time, he's galloping away from me.

12

Horse Show

The week of the horse show it seems like our whole town is getting ready for it. Colt and I help Mr. Harper scrub the boards and bars of the jumps they'll set around the fairground arena. Other kids in 4-H string up little white flags all the way around the horse show ring.

Every day after school Ethan and I do our homework. I write up two-thirds of my horse report—the failure of crying and begging. Then we bike to the cat farm to check on the pinto.

On Thursday, on our way to the barn, we're

passed by half a dozen small white trucks with fair foods written on the sides: lemonade, onion rings, elephant ears, Italian sandwiches, hot dogs. Only two more days until the horse show.

Mom's car is parked next to the barn when we get there. My first thought is that something has happened to the pinto. I jump off my bike before it comes to a stop. "Mom!"

Ethan drops his bike next to mine. He signs something, but I can't take the time to stop and see what he's saying.

"Mom, what's the—?" I ram into her just inside the barn.

"Whoa!" She puts her hand on my head. "What is it, Ellie?"

I stick my head around her until I can see the corner stall. The pinto is there, munching on grain. "I thought something was wrong. Why are you here, Mom?"

Mom steps aside. "I work here on Thursdays, remember?"

"Right. Thursday is cat farm day. Guess I forgot. I thought something bad had happened to the pinto." Still, I walk back to the corner stall to see for myself.

Ethan catches up to me. *That's what I was trying to tell you.*

I give the pinto a generous meal of Omolene. I like watching her go after it. But I can still count her ribs.

I pull out the hoof pick I bought at the supply store. I paid for it with my own money. "Guess I might as well clean out her hooves."

The pinto's ears flick to the sides. That means she's relaxed, and she stays that way even when I get in the stall with her. Her hooves are in great shape. Dad paid a farrier, the guy who takes care of horses' hooves, to come out and do a hoof trim.

He clipped the hooves so they're even all the way around, but he told Dad she didn't need shoes or anything else unless she'd be on gravel. All I have to do now is clean the gunk from the underside of the hooves. I use the pick to get at the V-shaped groove on the sole.

Ethan teaches me how to tie a slipknot with a quick release. In an emergency, I could yank the end and untie the knot.

When are you going to name her? he signs.

I put down the back hoof and take a minute before answering. It's not like I haven't thought about names. It's pretty awkward calling her "the pinto."

Finally I shake my head. "No name. I don't want us to get too attached."

Right, he signs, the smirk on his face speaking louder than his fingers.

When Mom finishes petting cats, she helps Ethan and me with the pinto's mane and tail.

Ethan signs to Mom, *Any news on a home for—* he glances at me and punches the air for the rest of his question—*THE PINTO?*

"I've got a lead on a nice shelter in Indiana," Mom reports. "And one in Virginia. I'd better find a spot soon, though. Mary Louise is as nervous as a turkey at Thanksgiving. She wants this horse off her cat farm."

✲ ✲ ✲

Friday before the horse show I end up sitting across from Ashley and Larissa in the cafeteria. I listen to their plans about which outfits they'll wear at the show. A bunch of the 4-H kids are entering the junior horsemanship class. It's the class with the biggest trophy. But everybody knows the winner will be Larissa or Ashley. Probably Larissa. She has won the last two years in a row.

Just when I'm sure Larissa and Ashley don't realize I'm at the table with them, Ashley turns to me. "Are you coming to the horse show, Ellie?"

"I never miss it." And that's the truth. Every year Colt and I watch it together. I hope he's planning to go again because I'm counting on catching a ride with him. My parents have to go to some Cub Scout thing with Ethan.

Larissa leaves without saying good-bye. Then again, I guess she never said hello.

Colt plops down beside me. "So, Ashley, can you beat Larissa this year?"

Ashley shrugs. "I haven't thought that much about it, I guess. I've been too nervous about riding Warrior in the jumper class. It's my first time jumping in a show."

"That is so cool!" I exclaim. It's hard not to be jealous of Ashley. Every single day I imagine riding my black stallion over jumps. But I've never actually jumped a horse.

"I think Dad is more excited about the horse show than I am," Ashley says. "Honestly, I think I'd enjoying watching more than showing."

Colt turns to me. "Are you going?"

I frown at him. "What do you think?"

He nods and walks off.

I catch up with him outside our classroom. "Colt! Are you going to the horse show or not? Can I ride with you?"

"'Course." Colt makes a face. "Girls," he mutters, shuffling into class.

"Boys," I mumblc, edging past him to get there first.

★ ★ ★

Saturday afternoon I wait outside for Colt's family to pick me up. I'm dressed in my cowboy boots, jeans, and a plaid Western shirt. If I can't be in the horse show, at least I can look the part.

Mom and Dad and Ethan file by me on their way to the car. I give Ethan a thumbs-up on his Cub Scout uniform. He gives me a thumbs-up on my cowboy gear.

"Are you sure you'll be all right until we get home?" Dad asks.

I point to the Stevenses' car backing out of their drive. "Here they come now." I wave good-bye to my family and jog across the street.

Colt motions me into the backseat with him. Mrs. Stevens is driving. No Mr. Stevens and no Sierra. "Thanks again for the lift," I tell her.

Colt's mom looks like she's going to a board meeting instead of a horse show. Her hair is twisted into a fancy knot, and she's wearing a blue suit with a straight skirt.

"You look nice, Mrs. Stevens."

"Thank you, Ellie," she says. "And you look . . . very horsey."

I'm not sure if that's a compliment, but I thank her just in case. "Isn't Mr. Stevens coming?" I'd ask about Sierra, but Colt's sister says horses are for little kids.

Colt's mom laughs—at least I think it's a laugh. Actually, it sounds a little more like a snort.

"Dad didn't make it home this weekend," Colt explains. "Anyway, he doesn't really like horse shows."

His mother mutters something under her breath, but I don't catch it. I think I'm glad I didn't hear.

Colt glances at me, then stares out the window. The sun is still out, but a bank of gray clouds is moving in.

"I sure hope it doesn't rain," I say. Four years ago the horse show got rained out.

I can't stand the silence in this car. I never know what to say around Colt's parents. Colt told me once that my parents are easier to talk to than his. Even for him.

"Um . . . it's nice that you like horse shows, Mrs. Stevens," I try. "I wish my parents did."

"Right," she says, giving me the same snort-laugh as before.

Colt explains in sign language, keeping his hands where his mom can't see in the rearview mirror. *Mom hates horses. She's only going because her boss has a daughter in the show.*

I nod. I'm pretty sure my dad doesn't know that Ms. Warden has a daughter in the horse show.

How come Mrs. Stevens knows about the boss's daughter and my dad doesn't? What else does she know that Dad doesn't? What else is she doing to make sure *she* gets that promotion and my dad does not?

13

Showtime

Mrs. Stevens turns us loose on the horse show grounds and tells us to come to the car after the show is over. That's the great thing about living in a small town like Hamilton. Our parents know that other kids' parents will keep an eye on us.

Colt and I leave Mrs. Stevens putting on more makeup in her rearview mirror.

"Let's claim our seats!" Colt shouts as he takes off running.

"Wait up!" I holler. "Let's check out the horses first."

He stops and comes back. "Good idea."

At least he's not dumping me for his buddies. Then again, Colt's buddies wouldn't be caught dead at a horse show.

We thread our way through the maze of horse trailers parked on the fairgrounds. Most of the license plates are Missouri and Kansas. But we spot Iowa, Illinois, and Kentucky too.

"There's Ashley! And her new hunter!" Colt leads the way to the Harpers' four-horse trailer.

The bay gelding is tied to one side of the trailer. He cranes his royal neck around, taking it all in. It's noisy around here, with horses neighing, people shouting, and music blaring from the speakers. But he doesn't seem nervous.

Ashley's hunter, Hancock's Warrior, is about the most beautiful horse I've ever seen up close. If he were black and a stallion, he might even be my dream horse.

Ashley steps out of the truck cab, where she changes her outfits for different classes. She looks like she's stepping off the cover of *Horse & Rider*. "Hi, Colt! Hey, Ellie. I'm so glad you guys came. I'm getting really nervous."

Colt and I tell her how fantastic her hunter is. We ask her about the classes she has entered. She answers all our questions, but I get the feeling we're more excited about the show than she is.

"Hey, you two!" Mr. Harper walks up, carrying two plastic cups. He hands one to Ashley, and she takes a sip. "Ellie, we were just talking about you," he says.

"About me?"

"I was thinking that maybe next year you'd like to ride one of our horses in the horsemanship class."

"Are you kidding?" I can't believe he's saying this. It wouldn't be the same as showing my own horse, but it would be pretty sweet. Every horse Mr. Harper owns is a show horse. Each one comes from a long line of winners. "That would be unbelievable!"

I glance at Ashley, and she's grinning. "Dad says you're his star pupil."

His star pupil? Even if they're just saying that to make me feel good, it works.

Then I notice Colt. "What about Colt, Mr. Harper?"

"I was just getting to that." He turns to Colt. "You've been doing great with Galahad. Do you think you'd like to work him on the barrels? See if you could get him ready by next year?" Galahad is their young quarter horse gelding. He's an easy ride, and Colt likes riding Western.

Colt's eyes shout, *Wow!* But he shrugs. "Sure. That would be all right."

"Good! You two keep practicing. By next year Ashley's going to have some stiff competition."

"Dad," Ashley scolds.

"I'd better get to work." Her dad disappears inside the trailer. When he comes out, he's leading Ashley's three-gaited mare, Cindy Lou. This is the horse she'll ride when she competes against Larissa and Custer's Darling Delight.

"We'd better go," I say because I know they need to get ready. "We'll be cheering for you."

"Thanks, you guys," Ashley calls after us.

As we leave to find seats, I try not to be jealous. I tell God I'm sorry for wishing I could be Ashley right now and have the horses she has. Even though God already knows how I feel, it helps me to tell him. Then I add, *And thanks for Mr. Harper wanting me to ride his horse. But would You please let me have my own horse to ride in the show next year?*

Right before the show starts, Colt points across the arena. "There's Larissa."

Larissa is decked out in an English riding habit. The number one is pinned to her shirt.

"I wonder how she managed to get *that* number," I whisper to Colt.

"Why don't you ask her?" Colt teases. "She's coming our way."

I can't believe it when Larissa crosses the arena and struts right up to us. She leans over the top rail and smiles at Colt. "Hi, Colt. Thanks for coming to watch me."

Larissa acts like she's only now noticing I'm there. "So, Ellie, I hear you're finally getting rid of that spotted horse."

14

Lost Again

"What did you just say, Larissa?" I demand.

"I said I hear you're getting rid of that spotted horse." This time when she says it, she makes a face like the words taste bad.

"What are you talking about?"

"They're shipping that nag out to some animal farm," she explains. "My uncle owns the trucking line that's supposed to haul shelter horses around. He told me that horse is bound for New Jersey."

"Wait." I try to wrap my mind around that. *New Jersey? Do they even* have *horses in New Jersey?* "I think you've got it wrong. My mom would have said something."

She shrugs. "Maybe she doesn't know yet. Whatever." She sticks a pin in her hair. "But they *are* getting rid of that spotted horse tomorrow." She starts off. "I have to go."

"Wait!" I want more details.

Larissa keeps walking.

"Why didn't anybody tell me?" I mutter.

"Why would they?" Colt asks. "It's not your problem."

"I know." In my mind I can see the pinto turning to watch me every time I leave the barn. I shove the picture out of my head, but it's hard to do.

"Ellie, what do *you* care?" Colt asks.

"I don't. You're right. I just wanted to make

sure the pinto was going to a good home. But it's not my problem."

"At least the horse isn't headed for animal control, right?" Colt waves across the arena. "There's Ashley!"

The first class is the Hunter/Jumper Youth class. There are only four entries, and Warrior wins easily. Ashley clears every jump except one.

Colt and I sit through the Western Pleasure Open, the English Pleasure Open, and the Twelve and Under Three-Gaited English Country Pleasure class, which Larissa and Custer's Darling Delight win. First out of a field of twelve.

Finally they call in the Twelve and Under Horsemanship class. This is the one where Larissa and Ashley ride against each other. I think it's the best class in the entire horse show.

As I've done every year, I imagine myself in the arena:

Ellie James rides in on her spirited coal-
black stallion. They trot as one around
the ring. The crowd . . .

Only I can't do it.

Every time I imagine myself on my dream horse, a horrible thing happens. He changes into . . . a pinto. The pinto.

I shake my head and try again . . . and again. But I can't get that scrawny pinto out of my head. It's no use. I can't stay here. Not even for the horsemanship class.

"Colt?"

"Shh. They're lining up, Ellie. The judge is about to—"

"I have to go."

He still hasn't turned around. "Go where?"

I stand. "Tell your mother I found another way home."

"What? Where–?"

But I don't stick around–not even to see who wins the horsemanship trophy.

I have to see that pinto one last time.

✭ ✭ ✭

By the time I reach the cat farm, it's getting dark. Swarms of cats prance out to rub against my ankles.

I listen for the pinto's nicker, but I don't hear it. "Hello? Pinto horse?"

No answer.

I pull the string for the barn's overhead light. Long shadows dance across the barn floor. Slanty cat eyes glow like fireflies on a dark night.

"Pinto?" I call, wishing I'd gone ahead and named her like Ethan suggested.

I walk toward her stall. The wood floor creaks with every click of my boots. "I'm coming, girl."

But when I reach the corner stall, she isn't there.

The pinto is gone.

15

Found Again

I stare into the empty stall. My heart pounds until my chest feels like it will burst. *It's not fair. They shouldn't have taken her away. Not before I could say good-bye.* Tears burn my throat and press behind my eyes.

Then I hear it. A soft nicker. It's coming from far away. From outside.

I race out of the barn. "Here, horse! Here, pinto!"

I tear around the back of the barn. And there she is! She's grazing, standing a few yards away.

There's no fence out here. Nothing to keep her from running away. I remember how much trouble we all had catching her at school. That day seems like months ago.

"Don't run off on me," I beg. I'm walking toward her, in spite of what I know about horses playing hard to get.

Instead of running, the pinto raises her head and nickers at me.

We step toward each other until I can take hold of her halter. "You had me so worried." I stroke her white blaze. It starts at the whorl between her eyes and goes down to her nose. It's jagged, like lightning.

"Why didn't I notice your blaze before? Funny. It was right there all the time."

It was right there all the time. The words echo in my head.

"Come on. Let's get you back to your stall."

I lead her into her corner stall. She doesn't fuss at all.

Once she's inside, I put down fresh straw. Then I give her an extra scoop of Omolene. "You need to look your best, pinto."

I run my fingers through her pure-white mane. Mom got all the burs out, and now the pinto's mane hangs down her neck in gentle waves.

"Yeah. Big day tomorrow. You're going to see your new home." I choke on the word *home*, as if there's something caught in my throat.

I get the brush and a clean rag and go to work on her coat. That same calico cat leaps onto the pinto's back and curls up there.

"You're a friend too, aren't you? Well, we have to help our friend make a good impression tomorrow. Right, Calico Cat?" I shake my head. "Listen to me—Calico Cat and Pinto Horse. Some names, huh? Sorry about that."

The cat purrs, a sound that might be a nicker if she were a horse.

I stroke the hairs on the pinto's black saddle spot. "You know, I think you've put on weight."

I run the cloth over her chest and legs. "You're a lot shinier than you were when I first *imagined* you at school."

While I finish rubbing her down, I tell her all about Larissa and Ashley at the horse show. Her ears prick up and rotate as I move around her. I pick out her hooves and fill her in on the promotion Colt's mother wants and my dad may want too.

"Don't tell Dad this, pinto, but I prayed he wouldn't get the promotion. I'd hate for him to be gone all the time. Do you think that's selfish? I guess a lot of my prayers are selfish. But I don't think God gets mad at me for it. Sometimes I imagine Jesus smiling at me while I pray, like He knows He's about to get another selfish prayer from Ellie, but He's glad I can be honest with Him. I'm glad too. Like how I ask God for a black stallion every night."

In my head, my own words are floating around again as if blown by the wind: *It was right there all the time.*

Outside it's dark as a black stallion at midnight. I'm not sure what time it is. But I know I'd better get home before Mom and Dad and Ethan get back and start worrying about me.

I give the pinto one more handful of Omolene. Then I hug her around the neck. "You'll be fine," I tell her. Only I can't hold back tears. It's stupid, I know. She's not my responsibility. She's not *my* horse.

I let her go. Then I leave the stall and don't look over my shoulder.

I head home, walking fast and trying not to

think. But pictures of the pinto flash through my mind. They're so real that I think I can hear her steps, those clumsy hoofbeats. And her nicker.

Her nicker?

I *did* hear her nicker!

I wheel around, and there she is. "You—you followed me?" Seeing her there, in the middle of the road, makes me laugh. I stroke her head with its white blaze. I scratch her behind the ears, under her halter.

With a deep sigh that starts in my boots, I whisper, "I have to take you back."

She doesn't pull away. She doesn't fight me when I lead her by the halter. "Did I forget to latch your stall, girl? I must not have been thinking straight. Guess I'm going to miss you just a bit."

I hate doing it, but I have to put her into the stall again. She stays put. Standing still. All alone.

I get her another handful of grain and then run out of the barn.

Even though my legs are tired from all the walking, I keep running. I want to get as far as I can from that barn. From the pinto.

I run until I'm out of breath and have to walk.

I'm almost back to town when I hear hoof-beats again.

It can't be. No way. I locked that stall. I know I did.

But when I turn around, there she is.

This time I burst into tears.

The pinto inches up the road toward me. She stops so close I can see the moon in her big brown eyes. And suddenly she looks beautiful. She's still scrawny. Her head is too big for her body. But her eyes . . . and her good heart . . .

It was right there all the time. "You! *You* were right there all the time!"

I throw my arms around her neck and let myself cry into her mane. "God answered my prayer, and I couldn't even see it." I cry and cry. And yet, somewhere during the cry, my tears change from sad to happy.

"You know what, pinto?" I tell her, wiping my tears on my sleeve. "It's a free country. If you want to walk with me, I can't stop you."

I turn and start walking. So does she. When I take a corner, she does too.

We walk like this all the way to my house.

When we pass Colt's place, he and his mom are pulling into their driveway. "Hey! Ellie!" Colt hollers out the window. "What are you doing with the pinto?"

I wave and shout back, "We're going home!"

16

Dream

The pinto follows me into the backyard. As soon as we're there, I see a small shadow moving behind us. Then a cat springs onto the pinto's back. The calico, of course.

"Like I told your friend," I inform the cat, "it's a free country."

The pinto drops her head and starts grazing like she owns the place. I could watch her eat all night. The big spot on her back that looks like a saddle still makes me laugh. I notice other spots—one on her leg that could be a star if it had another point. A triangle spot. An ear-shaped one on her chest. I love all of them.

I plop cross-legged in the grass and study her until I hear Dad's car pull into the garage.

Ethan finds me first. He runs into the yard, takes one look at the horse, then holds up his hands in the moonlight. *Somebody at Scouts said they were sending your horse away. I didn't believe it.*

My horse? I sign back.

He grins. He knew. Somehow, my brother knew.

Mom and Dad join us. I tell them everything about how the horse followed me home. Finally I get to the point. "Can I keep her?"

They look at each other. My parents have their own sign language. They talk with their eyes.

I watch them. This is the end of my report, the last third of the "experiment." No begging. No crying. Just prayer. Years and years of prayer. I'll turn in my report on Monday. And this is my ending. Horse or no horse?

When I can't stand it another second, Dad asks, "Where would you keep her?"

I wave my arm over the yard. "Right here. Ethan and I could help you build a fence. We've got plenty of room."

"Ellie," Mom says, serious now, "think about what you're doing. Didn't you want a fancy black show horse? That's what you've begged us for since you were knee-high to a grasshopper."

I nod. She's right. Only sitting out here in my backyard with the pinto, I've had a lot of time to think about that black stallion. "It's funny," I begin, trying to put my thoughts into words because it feels important to get it right. "I've begged, I've cried, and I've prayed that I could have a black stallion show horse. I even tried to get scientific about it for Miss Hernandez."

Mom and Dad exchange a frown and possibly a dozen silent questions and answers.

"But I finally figured it out." I reach up and stroke the pinto. "You're looking at the answer to all my prayers."

"The pinto?" Dad asks.

"The pinto," I answer, more sure than I've ever been of anything. "This is the horse of my dreams."

After a minute of silence from Mom and Dad, Ethan elbows me and signs, *What's her name?*

Without even thinking about it, I respond, "Ellie's Dream."

And the cat's name? Ethan asks.

"Her?" I answer. "Her name is Pinto, of course. Pinto Cat."

We all have a pretty good laugh at that one . . . except Dad.

My dad is gazing across our lawn. His head moves from side to side like he's watching a mower.

"So you want me to build a fence and whatnot all the way around the yard? It's over three acres back here. That's going to take some man hours. Good thing I'm not going for that big promotion at work, huh?"

"Really? You don't want the new job?" My whole insides relax. I guess I was more worried than I realized.

"Are you sure, Lenny?" Mom tosses some eye language at Dad and seems happy with his wordless answer.

I look around our giant lawn. Already I can imagine myself galloping Dream all over the backyard.

The backyard? I let out a laugh, remembering what Larissa said.

What's so funny? Ethan signs.

I can't stop grinning. "I just realized . . . we have ourselves an honest-to-goodness backyard horse."

God is able to do far more than we could
ever ask for or imagine. He does everything
by his power that is working in us.

Ephesians 3:20 (NIrv)

Horse Talk!

Bay–A reddish-brown color for a horse. A bay horse usually has a black mane and tail.

Blaze–A facial marking on a horse (usually a wide, jagged white stripe).

Canter–A horse's slow gallop; a more controlled three-beat gait.

English–A style of horseback riding that is often considered more formal and classic than Western style. Riders generally sit on a flat saddle, post (rise from the saddle) on a trot, and hold the reins in both hands.

Farrier–Someone trained to care for a horse's hooves. Farriers trim hooves and put shoes on horses, but many also treat leg and tendon problems.

Foreleg–One of a horse's front legs.

Forelock–The piece of hair that falls onto a horse's forehead.

Gait–The way a horse moves, as in a walk, a trot, a canter, or a gallop.

Gallop–A horse's natural and fast running gait. It's speedier than a lope or a canter.

Gelding–A male horse that has had surgery so he can't mate and produce foals (baby horses). Geldings often make the calmest riding horses.

Habit–An outfit for horseback riding or showing, usually including some kind of tailored jacket and hat.

Halter–The basic headgear worn by a horse so the handler can lead the animal with a rope.

Hand–The unit for measuring a horse's height from the withers (area between the shoulders) to the ground. One hand equals four inches (about the width of an average cowboy's hand).

Hindquarters–The back end of a horse, where much of a horse's power comes from.

Hoof pick–A hooked tool, usually made of metal, for cleaning packed dirt, stones, and gunk from the underside of a horse's hoof.

Hunter–A horse that's bred to carry a rider over jumps. In a horse show, hunters are judged on jumping ability and style.

Lead rope–A length of rope with a metal snap that attaches to a horse's halter.

Lope–The Western term for *canter*. The lope is usually smooth and slower than the canter of a horse ridden English.

Mare–A female horse over the age of four, or any female horse that has given birth.

Nicker–A soft, friendly sound made by horses, usually to greet other horses or trusted humans.

Pinto–Any horse with patches or spots of white and another color, usually brown or black.

Quarter horse–An American horse breed named because it's the fastest horse for a quarter-mile distance. Quarter horses are strong and are often used for ranch work. They're good-natured and easygoing.

Saddle horse–A saddle horse could be any horse trained to ride with a saddle. More specifically, the American saddlebred horse is an elegant breed of horse used as three- and five-gaited riding horses.

Shetland pony–A small breed, no bigger than 10.2 hands, that comes from the Shetland Islands off Scotland. Shetland ponies are the ideal size for small children, but the breed is known to be stubborn and hard to handle.

Sorrel–A horse with a reddish-brown or reddish-gold coat.

Stallion–A male horse that hasn't had surgery to prevent him from mating and producing foals.

Swayback–A sagging back on a horse, or a horse with a deeply dipped back. Being swayback is often a sign of old age in a horse.

Three-gaited–Used to describe an American saddlebred horse that has been trained to perform at a walk, trot, and canter.

Throatlatch–The strap part of the bridle that helps keep the bridle on. It goes under a horse's throat, running from the right ear and loosely fastening below the left ear.

Trot–The two-beat gait where a horse's legs move in diagonal pairs. A trot is generally a choppy ride.

Western–A style of horseback riding used by cowboys in the American West. Western horseback riders usually use heavier saddles with saddle horns and hold both reins in one hand.

Whicker–A low sound made by a horse. A whicker is sometimes thought to be a cross between a whinny and a nicker.

Whorl–A twist of hair that grows in the opposite direction from the surrounding coat. This patch is usually on a horse's forehead.

Withers–The top of a horse's shoulders, between the back and the neck. The height of a horse is measured from the withers to the ground.

Sign Language Alphabet

A		J		S	
B		K		T	
C		L		U	
D		M		V	
E		N		W	
F		O		X	
G		P		Y	
H		Q		Z	
I		R			

Acknowledgments

After this, my third animal series with Tyndale House, I think it's high time I thank my good friends who make up such a great team. To Katara Patton, acquisitions director for Tyndale Kids, thank you for your creative vision, for your wisdom, and for your godly guidance. To my gifted editor, Stephanie Voiland, you make work a joy—how I value your friendship! I'm also grateful to Cheryl Kerwin, Jackie Nuñez, Rachel Griffin, Erin Smith, and Tim Wolf.

About the Author

Dandi Daley Mackall grew up riding horses, taking her first solo bareback ride when she was three. Her best friends were Sugar, a pinto; Misty, probably a Morgan; and Towaco, an Appaloosa. Dandi and her husband, Joe; daughters, Jen and Katy; and son, Dan (when forced), enjoy riding Cheyenne, their paint. Dandi has written books for all ages, including Little Blessings books, *Degrees of Guilt: Kyra's Story, Degrees of Betrayal: Sierra's Story, Love Rules, Maggie's Story*, the Starlight Animal Rescue series, and the bestselling Winnie the Horse Gentler series. Her books (about 450 titles) have sold more than 4 million copies. She writes and rides from rural Ohio.

Visit Dandi at www.dandibooks.com.

ALSO FROM THE AUTHOR OF BACKYARD HORSES

Winnie
The Horse Gentler

1 **WILD THING**

2 **EAGER STAR**

3 **BOLD BEAUTY**

4 **MIDNIGHT MYSTERY**

5 **UNHAPPY APPY**

6 **GIFT HORSE**

7 **FRIENDLY FOAL**

8 **BUCKSKIN BANDIT**

COLLECT ALL EIGHT BOOKS!

CP0472